D1390382

Ms Wiz

AND THE DOG
FROM OUTER SPACE

Other books about Ms Wiz

Ms Wiz Spells Trouble

In Stitches with Ms Wiz

You're Nicked, Ms Wiz

In Control, Ms Wiz?

Ms Wiz Goes Live

Ms Wiz Banned!

Power-Crazy Ms Wiz

Ms Wiz Loves Dracula

Ms Wiz Rocks!

TERENCE BLACKER

Ms Wiz

AND THE DOG
FROM OUTER SPACE

Illustrated by
TONY ROSS

ANDERSEN PRESS
LONDON

This edition first published in 2010 by
ANDERSEN PRESS LIMITED
20 Vauxhall Bridge Road
London SW1V 2SA
www.andersenpress.co.uk

First published in *Totally Spaced, Ms Wiz* by Andersen Press in 2008

All rights reserved. No part of this publication may be reproduced,
stored in a retrieval system or transmitted in any form, or by any means,
electronic, mechanical, photocopying, recording or otherwise,
without the written permission of the publisher.

The rights of Terence Blacker and Tony Ross to be identified as the
author and illustrator of this work have been asserted by them in
accordance with the Copyright, Designs and Patents Act, 1988.

Text copyright © Terence Blacker, 2008
Illustration copyright © Tony Ross, 2008

British Library Cataloguing in Publication Data available.

ISBN 978 1 84939 157 3

Printed in China

To Lily Holbrook

Ms Wiz

AND THE DOG
FROM OUTER SPACE

CHAPTER ONE
PSYCHO PUPPY

Tilly Davis looked into her worm farm and sighed. There was no doubt about it, she thought to herself. Worms were not the greatest of pets.

With her finger, she gently turned the earth which she had gathered from the park and put into a plastic box to provide a home for her worms. Slither, the biggest worm, seemed to be asleep. So was Twisty, his friend. A smaller worm with a mark on its body, whom Tilly called Scar, moved slowly across the surface of the earth.

"Scar moved, Mum," Tilly called out.

Tilly's mother bustled into the room, brushing her hair, putting on her watch and talking all at the same time.

"We're both going to be late," she said. "If I tell my boss that I missed the train because Scar the pet worm had decided to move a bit, I don't think she'll be very impressed."

Tilly covered the three worms with earth. "Don't you listen to her, Scar," she whispered. "She loves you really. What was that?" She leaned forward and seemed to listen to what the worm was saying. "Scar says you work too hard, Mum. He says you should chill out like he does."

Mrs Davis stopped brushing her hair and looked at her daughter. "Maybe it's time to let those worms go," she said more gently. "They aren't really meant to be pets, are they?"

Tilly nodded. "I suppose they've had their adventure in the world of humans," she said, standing up. "I'll take them back to the park later today."

"Well done, love."

"And then I'll get some more worms."

Mrs Davis put her hand on Tilly's shoulder. "What about having a proper pet?" she asked. "A hamster perhaps. Or a lovely little guinea pig."

"I don't believe in keeping animals in a cage," said Tilly. "It's like putting them in prison."

"And we happen to live in a small flat on the fourth floor which is much too small for a cat," said her mother.

"What about a dog?" Tilly asked.

Mrs Davis winced. "They take a lot of time, you know, what with walks and vets and, I don't know . . . fleas and things. I'm a very busy woman and you're at school."

Tilly sighed and picked up the worm farm. "So," she said sadly. "Worms it is."

Mrs Davis glanced at her watch. "On your way, then. Jack and Podge will be waiting for you downstairs."

Tilly kissed her mother at the front door to their flat. Then, holding the plastic box in front of her, she made her way down the stone steps.

As she reached the landing below theirs, a door opened to the sound of snarling and snapping and two large dogs, tugging at their leads, emerged, followed by a big lumpy teenager who was struggling to control them.

"Hi, Nutter! Hi, Psycho!"

Tilly crouched down in front of the dogs. Seeing her, they began to wag their tails and whimper. Both of them licked her face – it was like going

through a very smelly car wash. She glanced up at their owner, who was called Gary but who preferred to use his nickname. "Hi . . . Gob," she said.

"You want to watch out for them dogs," he said. "They're killers when they get nasty."

Tilly laughed. "They're just telling me that they want to be let off their leads and have a run in the park."

"Yeah, like they really talk to you," said Gary.

For the briefest of moments, Tilly thought about telling him that it was true, that she really could understand what dogs wanted – it was as if she could hear their voices in her head. But then she realised that Gary would just think that she was a bit odd.

"'Bye, dogs," she said, then turned to make her way down the last flight of steps onto the pavement where Jack and Podge, her friends from St Barnabas School, were waiting for her.

It was not a perfect day at school. During the morning, Class Five's teacher Mr Bailey talked to the class about how the world's climate was changing. Lizzie, who was very interested in the environment, said that if the icecaps started melting, polar bears might become extinct.

Jack said that would be really lame because polar bears were his favourite animals.

Caroline said she preferred hippopotamuses, especially when they yawned.

"I've got an aunt who's got two parrots," said Podge. "They fly round the sitting room and hang off the curtain and do poos on the mantelpiece."

"Excuse me, Class Five, this is not pet corner!" said Mr Bailey, rather more loudly than he intended. "We're talking about the future of Planet Earth not about pets and their toilet habits."

"Tilly's got worms," thought Jack. At least, he thought he had thought it but, when he noticed that everyone in the class was staring at Tilly, he realised that he must have said the words out loud.

"Worms, Tilly?" Mr Bailey seemed to have forgotten about Planet Earth for a moment. "Is this true?"

Tilly was blushing. "What's wrong with having worms?" she muttered.

"That's quite enough of this discussion," said the teacher. "Tilly, the nurse is coming in this afternoon. Please tell her that you've got worms. She'll give you some pills."

"Pills?" said Tilly. "Why would I need pills?"

Mr Bailey seemed oddly embarrassed. "Well, sometimes if you eat something, these little worms can start growing in your stomach," he said.

"Tilly's worms are in a box," said Podge. "They're her pets and their names are—"

"Podge!" warned Tilly.

There was a moment of unusual silence in class.

"Perhaps we could return to the subject of global warming," said Mr Bailey.

After school, Tilly, Jack and Podge went home together through the park. When they reached a flowerbed in the park, Tilly put the worm farm on the ground, then gently turned it over so that the earth and her three worms tipped out.

"'Bye, Scar. 'Bye, Slither. 'Bye, Twisty. I'll miss you."

Podge put his hand over his mouth and squeaked, "And we'll miss you."

Jack nudged him in the ribs and frowned.

"Sorry, Till," said Podge. "See ya,

Twisty and the others."

They wandered towards the park gate in silence. On their way, Tilly noticed a small, wooden shed. She was just about to say to Jack and Podge that she had never noticed it before when something small, hairy and black and white appeared at the door of the shed and hurtled towards them. From the way that it nipped Jack's ankle, then Podge's, it seemed to be some sort of angry little dog.

"Ow!" shouted Jack.

"It's attacking me!" said Podge, doing a scared little dance.

The dog stopped in front of Tilly. It sat down, wagging its tail, and looked at her expectantly, one ear up.

"Where's that puppy gone?"

A woman in a long brown overcoat, holding a broom in her hands, appeared at the door of the shed.

"It's psycho, that thing," Jack called out. "You should keep it on a lead."

"She just chews through leads." The woman walked towards them, then looked down at the dog, which was

still gazing up at Tilly. "She chews through everything."

"Yeah, like my leg," said Podge.

"Come here, Thingy," said the woman.

"Thingy?" Jack said to Podge. "Bit of a funny name for a dog, isn't it?"

"Thingy!" the woman shouted. Then, sighing, she closed her eyes. A faint humming noise could be heard. As if being carried by invisible hands, the dog was lifted in the air and put down at the woman's feet.

As she leaned down to pat its head, Jack noticed that the park keeper was wearing black nail varnish.

"Ms Wiz?" he said. "Is that you?"

"Unless you know anyone else with a flying dog, it is," said Ms Wiz. "I said I go wherever magic is needed. The litter in this park is a disgrace."

"What's with the dog?" asked Podge.

"It was lost," said Ms Wiz casually. "I said I would give it a home."

From Ms Wiz's pocket emerged the head of Herbert, the magical rat. In each of his ears was stuffed some cotton. "Oh yes, and we don't worry about rats, do we? Because rats don't have feelings, do they? That horrible little Thingy is doing my head in."

For the first time, Tilly looked away from the dog towards Ms Wiz. "I know you're magic and all that but you really shouldn't call a dog 'it'," she said. "And Thingy's not a very nice name either."

Ms Wiz sighed. "I know it's not, but there was nothing on the list of names for the dogs of paranormal operatives that I particularly liked. I thought about Muttilda or Yapitha but they weren't quite her, somehow."

"She says her name is Ruby," said Tilly.

"Says?" Ms Wiz looked puzzled. "I know rats and cats can talk but Thingy – I mean, Ruby – has never said a word to me."

"Well, she's talking to me in my head," said Tilly. "She says she's called Ruby and she wants to find her mother."

Ms Wiz frowned slightly. "All right, I'll admit it. I'm impressed. I've seen all kinds of magic but I've never come across a psychic dog."

"Ruby says every dog can talk but that only a few humans can understand them. I happen to be one. And she really wants to know where her mum is."

"There is a bit of a problem there," said Ms Wiz. "Thingy – I mean, Ruby – has come from rather a long way away."

Herbert had pulled the cotton wool out of his ears. "There is absolutely no question of my returning to that horrible place," he said.

"Excuse me, Ms Wiz," said Tilly. "I thought you always said that you go wherever magic is needed. Just because it's a dog and not a human that needs help, you start making excuses."

"Yeah, but Ruby's mum could be anywhere in the world, right?" said Jack.

"Er, yes," said Ms Wiz quickly. "Almost right."

"And the last time she did a travelling spell, Class Five got stuck on the sunny tropical island of Sombrero," said Podge.

"And Class Four were turned into pigeons," said Jack.

"Almost right?" asked Tilly. "Why did you say that, Ms Wiz?"

"It's just a little thing," said Ms Wiz. "But in order to find Ruby's mother, we would have to cross the universe to a distant planet. There's just a possibility we might take a wrong turning and end up completely lost in space."

"Yeah, don't you just hate it when that happens?" said Jack.

"Poor Ruby," said Tilly. "She'll never ever see her mummy again."

Ms Wiz seemed to be thinking. "Oh, all right," she said suddenly. "Let's all go into space for a while."

There was a moment of

unenthusiastic silence in the park.

It was Podge who spoke first. "The problem is, I've got quite an important appointment. It's with some baked beans on toast back at my place."

"I've really got to do my homework," said Jack. "There's this really important geography project."

Herbert the rat wriggled out of Ms Wiz's pocket and down the leg of her trousers. "You can include me out, old girl," he said. "I do get so frightfully travel-sick."

"So it looks like just you and me then," said Ms Wiz to Tilly. "You hold on to one of Ruby's ears and I'll get the other."

"Are you going to freeze time while you step into another dimension?" Jack asked. "Otherwise Tilly's mum will be worried."

Podge groaned. "Why does time always stand still when it's time for my tea?" he said.

"There's no need for time to stand still," said Ms Wiz. "We'll be back soon enough." She closed her eyes and soon, all around them, could be heard a low humming noise. Gradually she and Tilly and Ruby faded from view.

Jack shrugged. "There's no talking to that Ms Wiz once she decides something."

"Well, at least I don't have to wait for my tea," said Podge.

"I think you do," said Jack, taking out his mobile. "We'd better call Mrs Davis and tell her that her daughter's in outer space looking for a dog."

From ground level, there was a small, polite cough. It was Herbert the rat.

"Ahem, I think you chaps may have forgotten something," he said. "All I'll be requiring is a nice warm armpit to sleep in and the occasional chocolate biscuit."

"Can't you look after yourself?" asked Jack. "Rats are famous for being able to survive anywhere."

"I think you might be mistaking me for an ordinary rat," said Herbert. "Now, be good lads and just pick me up."

Podge reached down for him and, before he could object, Herbert had wriggled between the buttons of his shirt.

"Aagh, it tickles," said Podge, writhing about a bit.

"Mmm." A muffled voice came from inside Podge's shirt as Herbert snuggled down. "Nice armpit."

CHAPTER TWO
ONE WEIRD PLANET

There are normally certain problems in travelling through space. You have to wear a spacesuit and helmet because there is no oxygen to breathe. You float about a bit because there is no gravity to keep you in your seat. If you go really fast, you can actually go back in time. In space, someone can pretty quickly become their own grandparent.

Fortunately for Tilly, magical space travel was different. It was simply a question of flying through the infinite blackness of the universe while holding on to a dog's ear and chatting as you go. As she, Ms Wiz and Ruby passed Mars, Ms Wiz was talking about her first pet, which had been a baby dinosaur.

"A dinosaur?" said Tilly. "You know, I had no idea that you were quite that old."

Ms Wiz smiled modestly. "I must say that I really don't look too bad for someone who has been knocking around since the beginning of time. You know what the secret is, Tilly? A sensible diet, lots of exercise and at least three spells every day."

Tilly gazed across the universe. "I've always wondered what it was like during the Ice Age," she said.

"Brrr." Ms Wiz gave a little shiver. "Don't even talk about it. But let me tell you about my pet dinosaur…"

And so, as they flew past Mars, Jupiter and Pluto, Ms Wiz and Tilly chatted about pets until they reached the planet where Ruby had once been born. The journey took a little over twenty minutes.

As they entered the atmosphere of the planet, the sky around them changed from black to a pinkish grey and then to a bright gold. As the three of them landed gently on some grass,

Tilly realised that the gold came from a warm and friendly sun above their heads.

She looked around her. There were fields, trees, the sound of birds singing. Ruby was so excited that she galloped crazily in circles, yapping with joy.

Ms Wiz looked around her and smiled. "I've always thought it was rather a nice place. It's called Planet Grrr."

"It's just like the countryside on earth," said Tilly. "Look—" she pointed to a hillside nearby "—I think I can see houses."

"That would be Grrrtown, the only town on Planet Grrr. It's where all the Grrrians live."

"Funny name, Planet Grrr," said Tilly. "Is there any reason it's called that?"

"Yes," said Ms Wiz. "As it happens, there is."

On the other side of the universe, Tilly's mother was panicking.

"Let me just get this right," she said when Jack telephoned her. "You're telling me that you met up with an old friend called Ms Wiz in the park, that she has magic powers and a dog from outer space and that she's now gone off to a distant planet with Tilly and the dog."

"That's about it," said Jack. "I'm sure everything will be fine. After all, Ms Wiz is a grown-up – sort of, anyway."

From Mrs Davis's handbag, came the sound of her mobile's ringtone.

"I've got a text," she said. "It might be her."

"Er, Mrs Davis. She's in outer—"

"'Bye."

Mrs Davis scrabbled in her bag for the mobile phone, then opened the text. It was from Tilly. She sighed with relief, then read what Tilly had written.

"gne in2 spce wth ms wiz. Bck sn. Txxxx."

Breathing deeply, Tilly's mother closed her mobile. "The important thing is not to panic," she murmured. "It's only . . . space, after all." She picked up the phone and dialled 999. "Hello, police," she said in a wobbly voice. "I'd like to report a missing person."

"So that's the reason it's called Planet Grrr," Ms Wiz was saying as they sat on a hill overlooking Grrrtown. "It's because the place is entirely run by dogs. Except on this planet they prefer to be called Grrrians."

"Weird," said Tilly. "And I can't believe that I can still text my mum from here."

"You couldn't in the old days," said Ms Wiz. "You had to use carrier pigeons. Now, thanks to modern magic, it's all much easier."

Tilly was wondering how exactly there could be carrier pigeons in space when suddenly she noticed some movement in the town. "There's a human over there!" she said. "So it's not just dogs."

"There are humans," said Ms Wiz carefully. "But they're not quite the same as us."

"They look the same," said Tilly.

"The humans here are actually pets,"

said Ms Wiz. "The Grrrians keep them for fun and for doing tasks. On Planet Grrr, humans are like horses for humans back on Earth." She stood up. "Perhaps we should take a closer look."

Under the gentle sun of Planet Grrr, Ms Wiz and Tilly walked slowly towards the town. As they approached, Tilly noticed that in front of each of the

little houses were beautiful wooden kennels.

In one street, the humans were making a new kennel for the dogs. Strangest of all, the humans were dressed exactly the same in a light beige tracksuit. At a park nearby, a group of humans were running around and playing, watched by three dogs who seemed to be talking among themselves.

"This is one strange planet," said Tilly.

"Yes, it is rather different," Ms Wiz agreed. "Look at the playground."

Tilly gasped. "It's for dogs!" she said. "There are balls everywhere and bones on strings that they can jump for. There's a toy cat that runs up trees. That's so sweet."

Ruby walked ahead of them and,

when Tilly called her, the dog ignored her.

"On Planet Grrr, humans follow dogs, not the other way around," said Ms Wiz, as she reached under a nearby bush and took out a small suitcase. When she opened it, there were two beige tracksuits. "Slip it on," she said. "From now on, we're Ruby's pets."

In their new beige pet uniforms, Ms Wiz and Tilly followed Ruby. When they reached the first house, Tilly noticed two humans in the back yard. They paced up and down the fence, saying, when they passed each other:

"Nice day."

"Nice day."

"Mustn't grumble."

"Takes all sorts."

Tilly shook her head. "It's like they can only do small talk – no real conversation," she said in a low voice.

"On Grrr, the humans just make friendly noises to each other," said Ms Wiz. "All the thinking is done by dogs."

Hearing them talk, Ruby turned and barked at them to stay closer.

"It's a nice place to visit, Planet Grrr," Tilly murmured under her breath. "But I don't think I'd want to live here."

CHAPTER THREE
WALKIES

"Jack Beddows and Peter Harris, also known as 'Podge'."

Sitting in an office at St Barnabas School, PC Boote made a careful note in his notebook. He glanced at the two boys sitting opposite him. They looked like troublemakers, he thought, but since they were the only witnesses to the disappearance of Tilly Davis, he had to take a statement from them. He wished he was out in a police car, chasing thieves with the light flashing and the siren going, like other policemen.

"All right, boys," he said. "Tell me in your own words what happened."

Jack and Podge took turns to tell the story of what happened in the park, as the policeman noted it down.

"Went to the park," he murmured as he wrote. "Buried some worms . . . Saw a small dog . . . Noticed the park keeper . . . Turned out to be Ms Wiz." At this point, PC Boote groaned to

himself. Whenever that Wiz woman was involved, trouble was never far away. "Decided to look for the dog's mother . . . Discovered it came from another planet . . . Tilly held its ears . . . Disappeared into outer space."

Slowly, PC Boote put his pencil back in his top pocket. "You should be aware, Jack and Peter, that wasting police time is a very serious offence – even if you are a bloomin' kid. You could end up in court."

"But they did disappear into space," Jack protested.

"Yeah, and I'm a Dutchman," said the policeman.

"Hm. The Dutch will be pleased." The voice – thin, posh and slightly muffled – came from the direction of Podge's armpit.

"What was that you just said?" PC Boote sat forward in his chair.

"Er, nothing," said Podge. "It's just that my armpit makes some funny noises now and then. It's a medical condition."

"Medical . . . condition." Because he couldn't think of anything to say, the policeman noted down the words. "Right. I have one last question. How did you know that the dog was missing its mother?"

Before either of them could answer, Herbert spoke from the direction of Peter's armpit. "Maybe it was feeling a little rough. Get it? Ruff! Ruff! Like a dog?" He chortled wheezily. "Sometimes I think I should be on the stage."

"Right, that's it." The policeman sprang to his feet. "I'm reporting you both for . . . inappropriateness. If I discover that Tilly Davis is not in space – which, frankly, I doubt very much – you both could end up in court."

Without another word, PC Boote stormed out of the room, walked quickly across the playground, jumped into his car and drove off with the tyres squealing.

"Oh dear." Herbert poked his head through the front of Podge's shirt. "Was it something I said?"

On Planet Grrr, things weren't going to plan either. Ruby lay with her chin resting on her paws in the kennel that had been found for her. Ms Wiz and Tilly were locked up with a few other humans in a house nearby.

Tilly had tried to talk to the humans but, although they seemed to understand, they would smile blankly and say something really boring, like "Turned out nice again" or "Takes all sorts, doesn't it?" or (a particular favourite) "Well, as long as you've got your health."

After a while Tilly gave up trying to talk to them. "The humans round here aren't exactly great at conversation," she murmured to Ms Wiz.

"They're pets," said Ms Wiz. "Their Grrrian owners don't like them to think too much."

Through the barred window, they noticed that Ruby was trotting towards the house. As she opened the door, the human pets began running about and jumping up and down in an excited way. Ruby barked once and the humans sat down, looking sorry for themselves.

She glanced towards Ms Wiz and Tilly.

"What's she saying to us?" asked Ms Wiz.

"Walkies," said Tilly.

Ms Wiz shook her head. "I really can't get used to being a pet," she said.

They followed Ruby out of the door and waited as she locked it behind her with her teeth. Then she looked up at Tilly.

When she had finished, Tilly turned to Ms Wiz.

"Ruby has been told that her mother isn't here," she said. "There's a rumour that she has been captured by the enemy."

"Enemy? Who could be an enemy of the Grrrians?"

Tilly frowned. "Cats," she said. "Ruby's mum has been captured by cats."

CHAPTER FOUR
A HISTORIC MOMENT
FOR RATKIND

Mr Harris, Podge's father, prided himself on being respectable. "I may not be rich and I may not be handsome," he used to say to Mrs Harris, "but at least I'm a respectable man. Isn't that right, Mother?"

"It certainly is," Mrs Harris used to say. "Respectability is your middle name."

So when his front doorbell rang and there, standing on his doorstep, was a policeman, Mr Harris assumed there had been a mistake. "Wrong house, young man," he said, making to close the door. "We're a law-abiding family here."

"You are the father of Peter Harris,

also known as 'Podge'?" said PC Boote in the deep, grown-up voice which he sometimes practised in front of the mirror when he was at home.

"I am," said Mr Harris.

"Then we need to have a little chat," said PC Boote.

The Harris family – Mr and Mrs Harris and, squeezed between them, their only son Podge sat on the sofa waiting

for PC Boote to find the right page in his notebook.

"I have made some very careful notes," he muttered. "It's just a question of finding them among the other crimes I'm working on."

"Crimes?" Mr Harris spoke sharply. "I'll not have talk of crimes in this house. Respectability's my middle name."

"Here we are." Smiling with relief, PC Boote smoothed down the page of his notebook. "I am currently investigating a very unusual case. Tilly Davis, young Peter's classmate from St Barnabas, has disappeared – allegedly to the other end of the universe."

"Other end of the universe?" said Mr Harris. "I've never heard such piffle—"

PC Boote held up a hand, as if he

was directing traffic. "Now we know that there has been text communication between Tilly and her mother. Mrs Davis asked Tilly where she was and received the reply—" The policeman checked his notebook. "'*Plnt Grrr*'." At this point in time, we do not precisely know what or where Plnt Grrr is."

"Plnt could be 'Planet'," suggested Podge.

PC Boote looked at him coldly, then smiled at his father. "We're not stupid down at the police station, Mr Harris. We know that nobody can text from the other end of the universe. It's way out of range. Unfortunately your boy and his friend Jack have gone along with this ridiculous story."

"But it's true," said Podge.

"And in addition," said the policeman, "your boy made some

extremely rude comments from the direction of his armpit."

"Odd?" said Mr Harris.

"Armpit?" said Mrs Harris.

Podge was just wondering how to explain what happened when Herbert the rat, who was under his shirt, made the decision for him.

"Can't *think* what the silly man's talking about," he said in a loud voice.

"There!" With a shaking hand, PC Boots pointed at Podge's armpit. "He's doing it again!"

"How on earth d'you do that, Peter?" asked Mrs Harris.

"It's a sort of magic thing," said Podge.

"Aha!" PC Boots leapt to his feet. "Now you're in trouble, young man." He thumbed through his notebook and took a piece of paper which he waved triumphantly. "This is an ASBO – an Anti-Social Behaviour Order. Normally ASBOs are to stop kids painting graffiti or vandalising property or frightening people. But this one's different." He glanced at the sheet in his hand. "It bans Ms Wiz, alias Dolores Wisdom, alias Diamante Wisporino, alias Dr Wisdom, alias Miss Wisbrowicz, from magic, spells or any paranormal—"

As the policeman was speaking, a long, loud and very rude noise came from Podge's armpit.

"Magic . . . spells . . ." PC Boote's normally pale face had gone quite red. "You're in breach of the ASBO. I'll take you down to the station, I will."

It was at that moment that there were signs of movement at the front of Podge's shirt. Herbert squeezed himself out and sat on Podge's lap.

Mrs Harris gave a little scream. "It's a rat!" she gasped.

"Calm down, young lady," said Herbert.

"A talking rat," said Mrs Harris, but then gave a little smile. "Did he say 'young lady'?"

"I am indeed a *talking* rat." Herbert gave a little bow in the direction of Mrs Harris. "It was not this charming young man who was doing the magic, but *moi*." He gave a little bow

"Herbert, the enchanted – the enchanting – rat, at your service."

"Herbert, this is my mum," said Podge.

"Your mother? Impossible. She's much too young and much too . . . slim."

"Oh!" Mrs Harris seemed to be blushing. "He's quite charming for a rat, isn't he?"

"I may be a rat, madam, but I can appreciate a beautiful woman when I see one," said Herbert.

"Do you—" Mrs Harris looked down, smiling shyly. "Do you really think I'm beautiful?"

Mr Harris pointed an accusing finger at Herbert. "Is that rodent flirting with my wife?" he asked angrily.

"That's just the way he is, Dad,"

Podge said quickly. "He likes to be polite."

PC Boote loomed over Herbert. "Do you belong to Ms Wiz?" he asked.

Herbert gave a little laugh. "If anything, she belongs to me. Frankly, I'm the brains of the outfit."

"In that case," said PC Boote, "I have no choice but to arrest you for committing magic in a public place."

Herbert held out his paws in front of him.

"Handcuff me then, officer," he said in a tragic voice.

"Take me to the cells. I shall be a martyr to magic.

'Tis a far, far better thing that I do—"

"Shut it, rat," said PC Boote. "Save your speeches for the judge." He turned to Mr Harris. "Would you happen to have some kind of box so that I can take the accused into custody?" he asked.

"We certainly do, officer. The sooner that rat's off the premises, the happier I'll be."

"I thought he was rather nice," said Mrs Harris weakly. "Lovely old-fashioned manners."

"Why couldn't you just keep your mouth shut for a change, Herbert?" Podge muttered to Herbert.

"I shall not be silenced," said Herbert. "There are times when even a rodent has to stand up for his rights. This is a historic moment for ratkind."

Podge shook his head. "Earth to Ms

Wiz," he murmured. "You're needed back here – urgently."

Crawling through the undergrowth on Planet Grrr behind Ruby the dog, Ms Wiz was thinking she would quite like to be back on earth, too. "Dogs in charge, cat terrorists, humans as pets," she whispered to Tilly. "Aren't you glad you don't live here?"

Ruby looked over her shoulder, baring her teeth slightly.

"She's telling us to be quiet," said Tilly. "We're getting near the cats' camp."

They stopped. Across a small valley, there was a small wood. In the low branches of the trees of the wood was an extraordinary sight. There were hundreds of cats of all colours and sizes. In a clearing beyond them could

be seen five dogs. As Tilly and Ms Wiz
watched, one dog tried to escape. The
cats let it run for a while, then
surrounded it.

"They're playing with the dog as if
it's a mouse," Tilly whispered.

Ruby whined.

"Perhaps Ruby could divert the cats'
attention," said Tilly. "Then we could
sneak round the back and—"

But Ms Wiz had stood up. "I think it's time to stop being a pet."

Ruby growled.

"She's telling you to sit," said Tilly.

But Ms Wiz was walking down the slope of the valley, then up the other side. As she approached, the cats turned towards her, ears back, hissing.

"Nice puss-pussies," said Ms Wiz. "Kitty kitty."

The cats crouched down, their hackles rising.

"Oh, suit yourself," said Ms Wiz. There was a low humming noise and suddenly, in the place of the cats, there were hundreds of mice.

"They've just learned an important lesson," said Ms Wiz as the mice scurried for cover. "It doesn't pay to mess with humans – especially paranormal ones."

A streak of black and white dashed past her into the wood. Soon Ruby and a dog that looked just like her were tumbling over one another yelping with excitement.

Moments later, Tilly arrived. "I think Ruby may have found her mum," she said.

CHAPTER FIVE
BIG PLACE, THE UNIVERSE

In Grrrtown, a group of dogs surrounded Ms Wiz and Tilly. There was growling, yapping, snapping and snarling. Now and then one of the larger dogs would bare its teeth in the general direction of Ms Wiz.

"Well, I must say, that's not very grateful." Ms Wiz was trying not to look scared. She looked down to their feet where Ruby and her mother, whose name turned out to be Grendel, were cowering.

Tilly was following the conversation of the angry dogs that surrounded them. "Some of the Grrrians are saying it was great that the cat terrorists have all been turned into mice and the hostages rescued but most of them are angry that it was a human pet who did it. And they're worried you might turn them into mice, too."

"They're right to be worried," said Ms Wiz. "I'm very tempted indeed."

As she spoke, a dangerous silence descended on the pack of dogs.

"Ah." Ms Wiz smiled as bravely as she could manage. "It looks as if the Woof Parliament has just managed to make up its mind."

Tilly didn't laugh. "Ms Wiz," she said urgently. "I think it's time for us to go."

The dogs moved closer, their eyes glinting, a low growl in their throats. Then, distantly, another noise – a sort of hum – could be heard.

"Very slowly," said Ms Wiz quietly, "lean down and hold Ruby's ears. I'll hold on to Grendel. Hang on." She closed her eyes. "I've just got to turn the mice back into cats."

When she looked again, the dogs were crouching, ready to pounce. The growling grew louder.

"Now, Ms Wiz!" screamed Tilly. "Now!"

Back on earth, Tilly's mother was just arriving at the police station, followed by Podge and Jack. In spite of the texts that she had received from Tilly, she was becoming more and more worried about her daughter being lost in space. Travelling across the universe accompanied by a paranormal operative and a dog just wasn't natural.

She pushed through the door of the police station and strode up to the desk where PC Boote was standing. "I believe you have arrested a rat," she said. "I need to talk to it."

PC Boote squared his shoulders. "I am not at liberty to divulge who is in custody at this police station, human or rat," he said.

"But we know he's here, constable," said Podge in his sweetest, most polite voice. "I saw you take him away in a shoe box."

PC Boote looked bored. "I repeat, I am not at liberty to—"

With a sudden movement, Mrs Davis reached out and grabbed the front of PC Boote's uniform. As she brought her face close to his she seemed to lift him off the ground. When she spoke, it was quietly and through gritted teeth.

"My daughter is missing, believed

lost in space. The rat knows where she is. We are going to talk to the rat right . . . now. It's really a very simple matter."

"B-b-but there's an ASBO." The policeman's eyes glanced left and right, looking for help. But he was on his own.

Mrs Davis tightened her grip. "D'you want me to get seriously angry?" she asked.

"Put me down," PC Boote said hoarsely. "And I'll take you to the rat."

Herbert was locked up in a cage on a table in a brightly lit room. He was not happy. As soon as Tilly's mum, Jack and Podge followed PC Boote through the door, he started complaining.

"I am not used to this treatment," he said in weak, tired voice. "It's uncomfortable. I can't sleep. There's no one to talk to. And the toilet facilities are frankly unforgivable."

Mrs Davis shook her head in amazement. "You were right, Podge. It really does talk," she said.

"That will be 'he', if you don't mind, madam," said Herbert.

"*He* would be well advised not to talk any more," said PC Boote. "A talking rat counts as magic in my book and right now magic is against the law."

"But if humans are allowed to speak, why can't I?" asked Herbert. "This is rattism, pure and simple."

Mrs Davis pulled up a chair and sat by the table so that she was at the same level as the cage. "Mr Herbert, we would like very much to know where Ms Wiz has gone with my daughter. All we know is that she's somewhere in the universe."

"Hmmm." Herbert scratched the side

of his nose. "Big place, the universe."

"Herbert," said Podge sharply. "This isn't a joke."

Suddenly the light bulb in the room flickered, then faded. For a few seconds, there was darkness. Then slowly, with a distant hum which grew louder and louder, the light returned.

The room was crowded now with two extra people. They were crouched on the floor and each seemed to be holding the ears of a dog.

"Ms Wiz!" said Jack.

"Tilly!" said Mrs Davis.

"Mum!"

For a moment, there was confusion in the police station. Tilly ran into her mother's arms. The dogs barked. Ms Wiz explained to Jack and Podge what had happened. PC Boote tried to keep order.

In his cage, Herbert closed his eyes wearily. "The same old Ms Wiz," he murmured. "She just has to be the centre of attention."

PC Boote moved purposefully towards Ms Wiz. From the top pocket of his uniform, he took out his notebook. "Ms Wiz, I am arresting you for committing magic in breach of your ASBO."

"Magic?" Ms Wiz looked puzzled. "Who on earth is Asbo?"

"As a specific example of the heretofore mentioned illegal magic, I have noted the following: being in possession of a talking rat—"

"Boooooring," Herbert sang out.

"—disappearing to the other side of the universe," PC Boote continued. "And appearing out of thin air in a police station without having first reported at the front desk."

Ms Wiz was smiling dangerously. "Is that all?" she said quietly. "I can do much better spells than that." A humming noise filled the room. PC Boote looked around, suddenly confused.

"What was I going to say?" He frowned to himself. "Why am I carrying this notebook? Why am I in a uniform? What am I doing here?"

"Your memory is now entirely blank," said Ms Wiz.

"But who am I?" said PC Boote. "I don't even know my name."

"Now." Ms Wiz ignored the policeman. "Let's get things sorted out. Herbert, you poor old thing." She opened the cage and held out her hand.

Murmuring, "You have simply no

idea what I've been through," Herbert wriggled into Ms Wiz's sleeve and up her arm, from where his muffled voice could be heard complaining. "She sugars off to the other side of the universe and does she give a thought for me? Not a chance. I'm just a rat, I'll be all right. It's just me me me with that Ms Wiz . . ."

"What are these dogs doing here?" asked Tilly's mother.

Ms Wiz groaned. "Why did I agree to bring them both back to Earth? I can't possibly look after two dogs."

At her feet, Ruby whined. Tilly listened for a moment, then whispered in her mother's ear. Mrs Davis glanced down at Ruby, who put her head on one side and cocked her ear as if waiting for a reply.

"Ms Wiz," said Tilly. "Ruby asked

me if she can come and live with us
and my mum, I think, has just agreed."

"And I would keep Grendel."
Ms Wiz smiled with relief. "It's perfect.
That puppy was exhausting me. They
can meet in the park now and then."

She knelt down beside Ruby.

"You stay here," she whispered.
"I'll see you soon." She held onto
Grendel's ear and closed her eyes.
A faint humming noise could be heard.

"Wait!" shouted Podge. "What about—?" He nodded in the direction of PC Boote, who was still looking about like a man lost in a maze.

Ms Wiz stood in front of him and looked into his eyes. "You are a community policeman," she said quietly. "Your name is Gavin Boote."

The policeman blinked twice, then sighed sadly. "Do I have to be?" he asked.

But Ms Wiz and Grendel were fading from view. Very faintly, a voice could be heard.

"See you in the park, Tilly."

There was a single bark of farewell from Grendel, and then silence.

On Planet Grrr, two human pets were talking.

"Nice day," said one.

"Mustn't grumble," said the other. "As long as you've got your health."

"Remember that human pet who came to visit – the one who rescued the hostages from the cats?" said the first.

"Yeah."

"Well, I've been thinking . . ."

Sophie
and the
Albino Camel

STEPHEN DAVIES

'Never mess with the Sahara Desert!'

That's what Sophie's dad is always telling her. But when Sophie meets Gidaado the Fourth and his fine albino camel, the offer of a camel ride is just too good to resist.

It turns out that the Sahara is more dangerous than Sophie could ever have imagined. There are snakes. There are djinns. There are sandstorms. And most terrifying of all there is Moussa ag Litni – a murderous Tuareg bandit intent on stealing camels.

'Pure adventure story . . . An exceptional short novel.' *TES*

9781842705513 £4.99

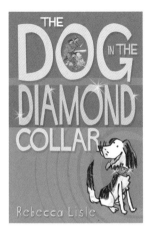

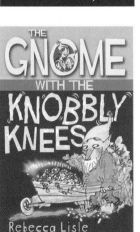

JOE, LAURIE and THEO STORIES

by REBECCA LISLE

with illustrations by TIM ARCHBOLD

Theo has a dog with a very special collar, and the two of them find gnome burglars, a boy lost in a magic box and a boy in a bear pit – all with a great deal of help from older brothers Joe and Laurie, naturally!

All £4.99

The Dog in the Diamond Collar
ISBN: 9781842703663

The Boy in the Big Black Box
ISBN: 9781842706817

The Gnome with the Knobbly Knees
ISBN: 9781842708897

Bobby and Charlton
stories by Sophie Smiley

with illustrations by
MICHAEL FOREMAN

Charlie's family are all football-mad. They always
work as a team, whether they have too much
snow, a fear of dogs, or are looking for a pirate
adventure. And the best player of all is Bobby,
who saves all the goals.

ISBN: 9781842701782

ISBN: 9781842704202

ISBN: 9781842706848

ISBN: 9781842708828

ISBN: 9781842708835

ISBN: 9781849390538

All £4.99

DAMIAN DROOTH SUPERSLEUTH

by Barbara Mitchelhill

with illustrations by Tony Ross

Detective work is Damian's thing, and he does solve all his cases, although he gets into an awful lot of trouble on the way! Read all the books and see how.

All £3.99

Disappearing Daughter
ISBN: 9781842705605

Popstar's Wedding
ISBN: 9781842705612

How to be a Detective
ISBN: 9781842705971

Spycatcher
ISBN: 9781842705674

Serious Graffiti
ISBN: 9781842706503

Dog Snatchers
ISBN: 9781842706497

Under Cover
ISBN: 9781842708255

Gruesome Ghosts
ISBN: 9781842708262

Football Forgery
ISBN: 9781849390354

AGENT Amelia

MICHAEL BROAD

Amelia Kidd is a secret agent, and her mission is to save the world. In fact, she's saved it loads of times from criminal masterminds. Read her secret case files, and find out all about it – available three in one book.

All £4.99

Ghost Diamond!
ISBN 9781842706626

Zombie Cows!
ISBN 9781842706633

Hypno Hounds!
ISBN 9781842708163

Spooky Ballet!
ISBN 9781842708170